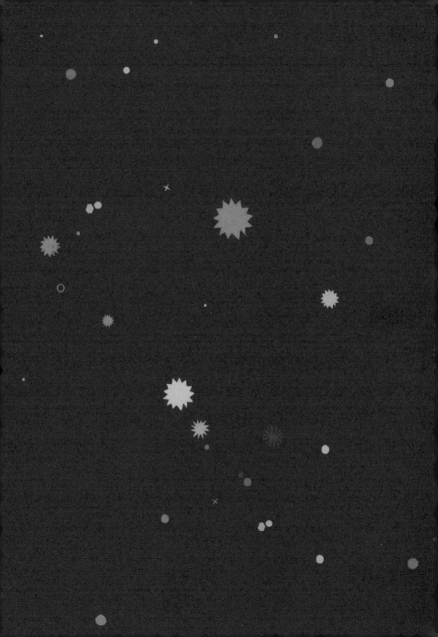

Grandpa Was an Astronaut

JONATHAN MERES

Grandpa Was an Astronaut

With illustrations by Hannah Coulson

Barrington Stoke

First published in 2016 in Great Britain by
Barrington Stoke Ltd
18 Walker Street, Edinburgh, EH3 7LP

www.barringtonstoke.co.uk

Text © 2016 Jonathan Meres
Illustrations © 2016 Hannah Coulson

A CIP catalogue record for this book is available
from the British Library upon request

ISBN: 978-1-78112-534-2

Printed in China by Leo

This book is super readable for young readers beginning
their independent reading journey.

 *To Ben and Rory*

CONTENTS

Chapter 1

Moon Thing

It was time to get up. So Sherman got up. Then he did some stuff. Here's a list of all the stuff that Sherman did –

1. Went to the toilet.

2. Washed his hands.

3. Splashed some water on his face
    to wake himself up.

4. Cleaned his teeth.

5. Took off his pyjamas and put
    some clothes on instead.

6. Went downstairs.

7. Said good morning to his mum.

8. Ate a bowl of cornflakes, with sliced banana but no sugar.

9. Told his mum that he wouldn't be long.

10. Went outside.

Sherman liked to be outside. He liked to be inside, too. But outside was best. Why? Because Sherman lived next to the sea in a small white house, with his mum and a dog called Luna. He didn't care about the weather. Hot, cold, windy, rainy or snowy. It made no difference at all to Sherman. He liked all kinds of weather. Well, most kinds of weather anyway.

But Sherman didn't like fog. Fog was rubbish, because when it was foggy, Sherman couldn't see things. And Sherman liked to see things as he stood on the shingly beach and listened to the waves slurp and suck at the shore. Things like distant ships, the water spouts of passing whales and clouds that looked like sharks.

But the thing that Sherman most liked to see was the moon. Whether it was hanging in the sky like a sideways silver smile, or whether it was full and round and peering above the horizon like a fat creamy cheese, Sherman liked to see it. And, if it was foggy, Sherman couldn't see it. That's why he didn't like fog.

Plus, when it was foggy, the foghorn in the lighthouse kept Sherman awake all night and made him grumpy the next day and his mum even grumpier.

But mainly it was the moon thing.

It wasn't foggy today. Today was sunny and fine and clear. Sherman could see for miles and miles, and so he was happy. But still not as happy as he would have been if he could see the moon.

Sherman had liked the moon for
as long as he could remember. Which
wasn't all that long because he was only
seven. But that was still quite a long
time to remember.

Grandpa said that the moon had
been full and round over a hundred

times since Sherman was born. And Grandpa should know. Grandpa knew loads of stuff about the moon. But then, Grandpa was an astronaut.

"Sherman?" Sherman's mum called from the back door of the small white house.

"Yeah?" Sherman called back from the beach.

"I need to see you!"

"But I've only just got here!" Sherman groaned.

"WOOF!" said Luna. "WOOF! WOOF!"

"Coming!" said Sherman.

Chapter 2

Many Moons Ago

"Hey, guess what?" Sherman's mum said when Sherman got back to the small white house.

"What?" said Sherman. He wasn't very good at guessing things.

"Grandpa just called."

"Really?" Sherman said, and his face lit up like someone watching a firework.

Sherman's mum nodded.

"And?" Sherman said. He wondered if this was the only reason he'd been called back from the beach.

"He wants us to go and see him."

"He does?" Sherman said, and his eyes twinkled like stars.

Sherman's mum nodded again.

"When?" said Sherman.

"Today," said Sherman's mum. "Right now in fact."

"YEEEEEEEEEEEEEEEAH!!!" Sherman yelled, and he did a dance that he only ever did when he was very happy. Because there was only one thing that Sherman loved more than having a grandpa who was an astronaut. And that was going to see him.

Of course, Grandpa wasn't still an astronaut. He'd stopped a long, long time ago. Or, as Grandpa would say, many moons ago. But he'd been an astronaut once upon a time, when he was much younger. Before he'd met Grandma and long before Sherman's mum was born.

Many moons ago, astronauts were celebrities. They were like pop stars, movie stars and famous footballers, all rolled into one. But these days, Grandpa could sit in a café drinking a coffee and reading his newspaper and no one would know who he was. This was fine by Grandpa, because Grandpa didn't like a lot of fuss and bother. To Grandpa, being an astronaut was just another job and no more special than fixing washing machines, or driving buses.

Sherman kind of knew what Grandpa
meant. He also kind of knew that being
an astronaut really was special, but
that Grandpa didn't like to show off. But
Sherman thought that Grandpa should

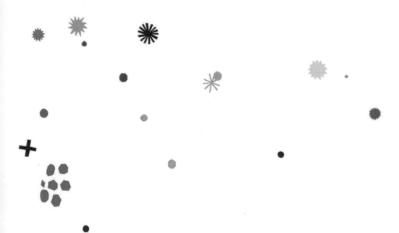

show off. After all, it wasn't everyone who could say that they'd floated about on the moon. Only a few people in the world could say that. And Grandpa was one of them!

"Let's go," Sherman's mum said, and she bundled Sherman and Luna into the car.

And off they went.

Chapter 3
Real Moon Rock

When Grandpa opened the door and saw Sherman, he said what he always said.

"Grandpa to Sherman! Grandpa to Sherman! Come in please, Sherman!"

Sherman laughed like he always did. Sherman loved it when Grandpa said stuff like that. Stuff that he used to say back when he was an astronaut. And when he said it, Grandpa always covered his nose and mouth with his hand, so that his voice sounded all funny and muffled. As if he was far, far away, zooming through space.

"Are you receiving me, Sherman?" Grandpa said.

"Receiving you loud and clear, Grandpa," said Sherman.

"In that case, what are you waiting for?" Grandpa said. "Come in!"

When Sherman stepped inside Grandpa's house he did what he always did and headed straight for the mantelpiece. There were two things there that Sherman liked to look at.

First of all there was the photograph.
Not just any old photograph. A
photograph of Grandpa standing on
the moon, next to a flag he'd just stuck
in the ground. Of course you couldn't
really tell that it was Grandpa because

Grandpa was wearing his special space suit and his big round helmet. You couldn't see his face. But Sherman knew that it was Grandpa, because Grandpa said it was. And that was good enough for Sherman.

The other thing on the mantelpiece that Sherman liked to look at was a small glass case. In the case was a tiny lump of rock. Not just any old rock. Real moon rock. Dusty and white. Not in the least bit like cheese. That was just a kids' story. Same as all that "hey diddle diddle" stuff and cows jumping over the moon. Sherman knew that none of that was true.

"What's it like on the moon, Grandpa?" Sherman said when Grandpa came and stood beside him.

"Let's find out, shall we?" said Grandpa.

"Pardon?" said Sherman.

"Let's find out," said Grandpa again.

"How will we do that?" Sherman asked.

"We'll go there," Grandpa said, with a shrug of his shoulders, as if he'd just suggested they go to the swing park, or the swimming pool.

"Whoa!" said Sherman. "Really?"

"Really," Grandpa said.

"How?" Sherman asked.

"We'll build a spaceship," said Grandpa.

"Cool," said Sherman.

And so they did.

Chapter 4
Blast Off

It turned out to be much easier to build a spaceship than Sherman thought it was going to be. All it took was a few cardboard boxes, a dustbin lid, a couple of chairs and some silver foil.

"See?" said Grandpa, as he and Sherman stood back and admired their handiwork. "It's not exactly rocket science."

Sherman laughed in case it was a joke. He was pretty sure that it was, because Grandpa was always making jokes about space.

Like ...

'What do you do if you see a
spaceman?'

'You park, man.'

And ...

'Why are there never any parties on the moon?'

'Because there's no atmosphere.'

Sherman didn't always understand Grandpa's jokes. But he didn't care. They were Grandpa's jokes. So they must be funny.

"All set?" Grandpa said.

"All set," said Sherman.

"Hop in then," said Grandpa, and he stepped inside the spaceship.

"Roger," Sherman said, and he hopped in. Sherman knew that's what astronauts said instead of "OK". They said "Roger" even if the person they were speaking to wasn't called Roger.

"You coming, Luna?" Grandpa said.

"WOOF!" said Luna. Her tail wagged like a windscreen wiper as she jumped into the spaceship and landed at Sherman's feet.

"Prepare for blast off," Grandpa said. "Are you receiving me?"

"Receiving you loud and clear," said Sherman.

"Commencing countdown, engines on," Grandpa said.

"Roger," said Sherman.

"Ten ... nine ... eight," said Grandpa.

"Seven ... six ... five ... four," said Sherman.

"Three ... two ... one ... zero!" said Grandpa.

"BLAST OFF!" Sherman and Grandpa
yelled together.

The house shook and shuddered as Grandpa, Sherman and Luna blasted off for the moon. In next to no time they'd burst out of the clouds and they were zooming through space at an amazing speed. Soon Planet Earth looked as tiny as a golf ball below them.

"Are we there yet, Grandpa?" said Sherman.

Grandpa roared with laughter. "Are we there yet?"

Sherman nodded.

"Do you know how long it took me to get to the moon?" said Grandpa.

Sherman shook his head.

"Three days," said Grandpa.

"Whoa!" Sherman said. "Three days?"

"I know," said Grandpa. "Imagine that."

So Sherman did.

Chapter 5
One Small Step for Dog

When at last they reached the moon, the spaceship landed with a soft bump.

"We have touchdown," said Grandpa.

"Cool," Sherman said.

"WOOF!" said Luna.

"After you," said Grandpa.

"No, after you, Grandpa," Sherman said. "I insist."

"WOOF! WOOF!" said Luna. She was unable to wait a second longer and jumped out of the spaceship.

"That's one small step for dog," said Grandpa. "One giant leap for dogkind."

Sherman wasn't sure if this was another one of Grandpa's jokes or not, but he laughed all the same.

"Ready?" said Grandpa.

"Roger," said Sherman.

"Let's go!" said Grandpa.

Grandpa and Sherman stepped off the spaceship. There's no gravity on the moon and so they floated and bounced around. Sherman was pretty sure it was

the best fun he'd ever had. Much more
fun than any bouncy castle he'd ever
bounced on, or any soft play centre he'd
ever played in.

"WHEEEEEEEEEE!" went Sherman.

"WHEEEEEEEEEE!" went Grandpa.

"WOOOOOOOOOF!" went Luna.

But all that floating and bouncing about was thirsty work. The problem was they'd forgotten to bring anything to drink. The situation soon became grave.

"Houston, we have a problem," Grandpa said. He sat down and scratched his head.

"Look, Grandpa!" said Sherman as all of a sudden Sherman's mum appeared in another spaceship with emergency supplies of lemonade and biscuits.

"That was touch and go there for a while," said Grandpa.

MUM'S
SPACEY
SNACK
SHUTTLE

"Are you OK, Dad?" said Sherman's mum.

"Of course I'm OK." Grandpa laughed, glancing at Sherman. But Sherman hadn't even heard his mum. He was much too busy slurping lemonade and munching biscuits.

"You're not overdoing it, are you?" Sherman's mum said.

"Of course not," said Grandpa. "Stop fussing."

As if to prove that he was fine, Grandpa stood up and did a funny floaty dance. Sherman laughed so much he almost spat out a mouthful of lemonade.

"Don't be long now," Sherman's mum said as she blasted off again. "It's nearly time for us to go."

"Go where, Mum?" said Sherman.

"Home!" Sherman's mum yelled as she zoomed back towards Earth.

"Aw," Sherman wailed. "Do we have to go?"

Grandpa smiled. "We've all got to go home sometime, Sherman."

Sherman sighed. "Suppose so."

"Ten ... nine ... eight ..." said Grandpa.

"Wait!" Sherman said. "Luna?"

"WOOF! WOOF!" said Luna as she jumped back into the spaceship just in the nick of time.

"Seven ... six ... five ... four ..." said Grandpa.

"Three ... two ... one ... zero," said Sherman.

"BLAST OFF!" Sherman and Grandpa said together.

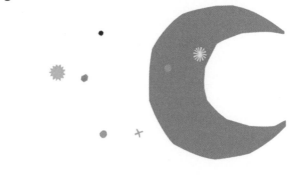

Chapter 6

Waxing and Waning

Sherman and Grandpa landed back on Earth just in time for tea. They tucked into their sausage, chips and peas, as a happy Luna wolfed down a big bowl of dog biscuits.

Afterwards they went outside and gazed up into the night sky. The moon shone down more brightly than Sherman had ever seen it shine before. It was almost dazzling.

"Grandpa?" Sherman said.

"Yes?" said Grandpa.

"Why is the moon round sometimes and then other times it's like ..."

"Like what?" said Grandpa.

Sherman thought for a moment. "A banana."

Grandpa laughed. "That's called a crescent moon."

"Oh," said Sherman.

"The moon doesn't really get bigger and smaller," Grandpa said. "It just seems that way when we see it from down here."

"Right," said Sherman.

"It's called waxing and waning," Grandpa said. "Waxing is when it's getting bigger and waning is when it's getting smaller."

"Cool," said Sherman.

"Just like you and me, Sherman."

Sherman pulled a puzzled face. "What do you mean, Grandpa?"

Grandpa smiled. "Well, you're waxing and I'm waning."

"I don't understand," said Sherman.

"You're getting bigger and I'm getting smaller."

Sherman burst out laughing. "Don't be silly, Grandpa! You're not getting smaller!"

Grandpa put his arm around Sherman and gave him a squeeze.

"Grandpa?"

"Yes, Sherman?"

"Do you think you'll go back to the moon one day?"

"You mean the real moon?" said Grandpa.

Sherman nodded.

"Sure I will," said Grandpa.

"When?" Sherman asked.

"I don't know," said Grandpa. "Some day soon."

"Sherman?" Sherman's mum called from the house.

"Yes, Mum?" Sherman called.

"We're leaving!"

"Aw," said Sherman.

Chapter 7
Over and Out

"Have you had a good day, Sherman?"
Grandpa asked as Sherman climbed into
the back of the car.

"The best day ever," Sherman said.

"Me too," said Grandpa.

"Really, Grandpa?" Sherman said.

"Really," said Grandpa.

"Even better than the day you really went to the moon?" said Sherman.

Grandpa laughed. "Even better than that!"

Sherman's mum smiled as she turned the key and the car spluttered to life.

"Close the door, Sherman," she said.

Sherman closed the door and fastened his seatbelt.

"Wait there!" Grandpa shouted. "I'll be back in a minute!"

Grandpa hurried into the house and reappeared a few moments later carrying a small cardboard box.

Sherman pushed the button that made his window go down.

"I've been thinking about what you asked me," Grandpa said. "About going back to the moon some day?"

Sherman looked at Grandpa.

"I'll need you to look after a couple of things while I'm gone, Sherman. Are you receiving me?"

Sherman nodded. "Receiving you loud and clear, Grandpa."

"Excellent," Grandpa said, and he handed the box over to Sherman.

Sherman opened the box to see what the couple of things were.

To his amazement one was the photograph of Grandpa standing on the moon. The other was the moon rock in the small glass case.

"You will take care of them now, won't you?" Grandpa said.

"Roger," said Sherman.

"Say goodbye to Grandpa, Sherman," Sherman's mum said.

"Bye, Grandpa!" Sherman called as the car set off down the road.

"Bye, Sherman!" Grandpa called. "Over and out!"

"Over and out!" called Sherman.

"WOOF!" said Luna.

Sherman turned around to look through the rear window. Already Grandpa was as tiny as a golf ball. Then the next moment they turned a corner. And Grandpa was gone.

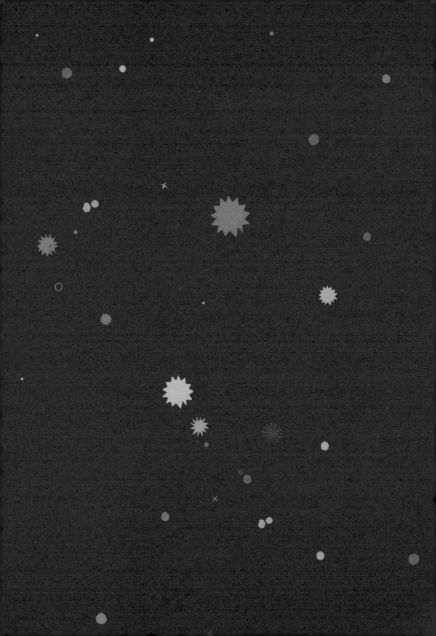